SLAIN IN SCOTLAND

RAMBLING RV COZY MYSTERIES, BOOK 15

PATTI BENNING

SUMMER PRESCOTT BOOKS PUBLISHING

CHAPTER ONE

"This must be it."

Tulia leaned forward in her seat, peering out the windshield of their rental car to get her first look at the little bed and breakfast, which was nestled on the rocky shore of Loch Uiginn in Scotland. It was an old-fashioned stone house with a wooden sign blowing gently in the breeze that read *Uiginn House Bed & Breakfast*. A couple of other small cars were parked in the gravel lot out front. Samuel pulled their rental vehicle to a stop in a parking spot close to the front door.

"It looks so cozy," Tulia said. "I'm glad we decided to do this. It will be nice to relax for the last week of our trip."

They were on the last week of their tour of

Europe. It was Tulia's first time out of the country, and so far, she had enjoyed every minute of it. They had flown into France, and had spent a few days in Paris before exploring the French countryside. After that, they had taken a train through Belgium to Germany, where they stayed in a cozy inn in Frankfurt, before moving on to Cologne. Then they traveled through the Netherlands before taking a boat to the UK. They were just coming from a few days in London, and so far their trip had been fun, but a whirlwind of constant activity.

They were both looking forward to relaxing somewhere scenic for the rest of their vacation. It had been fun traveling in places where she had to refer to a language dictionary to get her point across — though, a surprising number of people had spoken English everywhere they went – but while the rural accents here in the UK could be a little hard for her to understand sometimes, it would be a lot easier to spend a quiet week somewhere everyone spoke the same language.

"The email said check-in was at eleven, so our room should be ready for us," Samuel said. "Do you want to go in together? We can bring our things up once we know exactly where we're going."

"Sounds good to me," Tulia said, unbuckling her

seatbelt. It still felt odd to have the passenger seat on the left-hand side of the vehicle. She had tried her hand at driving on the left side of the road, but still wasn't comfortable with it. Thankfully, Samuel had picked up the skill a lot more quickly than she had. She was glad to have him be the one to drive and figure out all of the foreign road customs instead of her.

As she got out of the car, something large, yellow, and furry came bounding around the corner of the bed and breakfast. A huge golden retriever, dripping wet, paused right in front of her and then shook the water off its fur, sending a spray of droplets through the air. A second one joined it from around the back of the building. Tulia held out her hands as the two large, fluffy dogs sniffed her legs, their tails wagging back and forth slowly as they examined her. Finally, one of them leaned into her side and enjoyed a few moments of her scratching behind its ears while the other dog went over to Samuel for a similar greeting.

"I like this place already," he said, grinning. "I wonder if they belong to the woman who owns this place, or if they are a guest's dogs."

"I have no idea, but they sure are cute." She felt a twinge in her heart. "It makes me miss Cicero, though. I really owe Violet for watching him all this time."

"She doesn't mind," Samuel assured her. "I'm glad he gets along with her and Marc. I know it must have been difficult to leave him for so long."

"I wish I could have brought him," she admitted as she grabbed her purse, gently pushed one of the dogs away from the open car door, then shut the vehicle. "There is no way he could have gotten through customs, though. It would have been hard enough with a dog. I just hope he knows I haven't abandoned him."

"You've been video calling him," he reminded her. "I'm sure he understands that you're coming back. It's not the first time you've left him to go on a trip. Plus, you know Violet and Marc are spoiling him."

She chuckled. "I know. He's going to weigh twice as much as he did when I left by the time we get home."

With the dogs following them, they headed up to the bed and breakfast's door. Samuel opened it and they stepped inside. The interior was dim, but cozy, with a woven rug on the hardwood floor and a vase of wildflowers at the front desk. The sound of rustling pages caught Tulia's attention, and she glanced to the right to see a man with sandy blond hair sitting at a small table in a reading nook, his laptop open in front of him as he flipped through some printed pages of paper. He glanced up and nodded at them, but didn't get up to greet them so she figured he was another guest and not an employee.

The dogs filed past them, one of them going over to a half full food bowl on the ground next to the desk. The other one flopped down on a large, plush dog bed in the corner.

"They must belong to the owner," Tulia murmured.

"There's a bell to ring for service," Samuel said. It was an old-fashioned one, the sort he had to pick up to ring. After ringing it, they waited only a moment before they heard someone coming down the hallway.

"Just a second," a woman called out. "I'll be right there."

A middle-aged woman with her hair pulled back in a long, greying braid came down the hall, a pile of freshly folded towels in her arms. She set those on the edge of the front desk, then stepped around behind it.

"Welcome to the Uiginn House. Do the two of you have a reservation with us?"

"Yes," Tulia said. "It should be under Blake. Tulia and Samuel. We're here for the week."

"Yep, I have you right here," the woman said, nodding at her computer. It looked ancient, but seemed to work well enough as she tapped a few keys, and then opened the drawer to take out an old-fashioned keyring. "I'm Gwen, by the way. I have the two of you on the second floor. I hope that's all right. I'll show you around briefly. Will you need any help bringing your things in? Ewan is around here somewhere, but I'm not sure where he got to. I might have to hunt him down for you."

"We should be fine," Samuel said. "This is a nice place you have here."

"And nice dogs," Tulia said with a smile.

Gwen chuckled. "I see you met Heather and Honey. They're good girls. They love swimming in the loch. There are toys around back if you want to play fetch with them, and feel free to give them treats from the bowl on the desk. We don't allow them in the guestrooms, though. Just shoo them away if they try to follow you in. If they bother you, let me know. They're used to having guests around. They love the attention."

"We don't mind them at all," Samuel said as Gwen came out from behind the desk. They followed her up the stairs.

"We're just about full-up this week. You'll have a

man, Matthew, in the room next to yours. Downstairs is another couple, Chloe and Ryan. And then we've got a backpacker, Christopher, who is sleeping out in the carriage house in exchange for a bit of work. They're a good group, and I'm sure you'll fit right in. You're welcome to go off and do your own thing, of course, but we do have some group activities as well, and we all eat supper together in the dining room each evening."

"That sounds perfect," Tulia assured her as Gwen unlocked the door. She pushed it open and stepped back, handing them the key ring.

"Well, this is yours for the week. Make yourselves at home. If you need anything at all, come find me or Ewan. You'll recognize him straightaway. He has short black hair and he'll have a name tag on. He is our main helper around here. Oh, before I forget, there's a boat tour leaving tomorrow morning. It'll take you around the loch, and the captain will tell you the history of the fort on the far shore. Lunch is provided. The man who owns the boat is a neighbor of mine, and he does this every week as a favor to me. So, it will just be the group from the bed and breakfast. I think everyone else is going. Should I jot your names down too? I need to know how many sandwiches to make."

Samuel and Tulia glanced at each other, immediately in agreement. Tulia smiled. "That sounds lovely. We'll go."

Gwen smiled at them. "Wonderful. I'll put you down. You get settled in, now. I hope you enjoy your stay."

The room was cozy, with a soft green quilt on the bed, a picture of the loch hanging on the wall, and a cozy loveseat in front of a small table on the other side of the room. There was an attached bathroom, which was a bit dated but perfectly serviceable, and the window looked out over Loch Uiginn in the back of the bed and breakfast.

"It's beautiful here," Tulia murmured. She turned away from the window and then froze, seeing that Samuel had dropped to one knee behind her, a small black velvet box in his hand.

"I know we've only talked about this a little," he said. "And we haven't been dating for quite a year yet, though we have known each other for longer than that. But I'm certain I want to spend the rest of my life with you, Tulia. If you feel the same way, I would be honored if you would agree to be my wife."

She gasped, staring at him with wide eyes. After a second, she realized he was waiting for a reply and she said, "Yes! Samuel, my goodness, yes."

He rose and pulled her into a hug before drawing back slightly to kiss her. She watched as he put the ring on her finger, admiring the sparkling diamond and the white gold band.

She had been on a lot of wonderful trips in her life so far, but she knew that this one would always hold a special place in her heart, because it was where she had gotten engaged.

CHAPTER TWO

With the excitement of the proposal, it took them a while to get around to bringing in their luggage. Gwen popped by to tell them that dinner would be served soon just as they were finishing up their unpacking. Tulia changed into a cozy sweater, since it was starting to get a little chilly out, and the two of them went downstairs hand in hand. Whatever Gwen had made for dinner smelled amazing, and she felt her stomach rumble. She hadn't even thought about food until now, what with the excitement of being engaged.

A man who must have been Ewan, since he matched Gwen's description of her employee, guided them into the dining room, where a long, wooden table was already set with the supper setting. A pot of stew, a plate of roast potatoes, and freshly made dinner rolls took center stage, along with a salad and some fresh fruit. She and Samuel were the last to arrive. Before they ate, Gwen asked everyone to go around and introduce themselves. Tulia and Samuel started, and she was thrilled to introduce him as her fiancé, grinning like mad the whole time.

Next was the man seated next to them, who introduced himself as Matthew. "This is my first time out of the country. I just came into an inheritance, and I knew I wanted my first big expense to be a trip like this. I think I'm in the room next to yours," he said. "You're American too?"

Samuel nodded. "We're from the Boston area."

"Oh, nice. I'm from New York. Not the city, I live in a small town upstate."

"We're from California," a woman across the table from Tulia said. "My name is Chloe. And this is Ryan, my boyfriend." They were both young, in their mid-twenties. Chloe's auburn hair was cut in a short bob, and Ryan's was long enough to be up in a pony-tail. They looked cheerful, and Tulia was looking forward to talking to them about where else they had been. She had enjoyed her time on the West Coast.

The last guest introduced himself as Christopher. He was the only non-American guest there.

"I'm a backpacker from just outside of London,"

he told them. "I suppose you could call this an early midlife crisis. I decided to see the country while I figure out what I want to do with my life."

He looked remarkably similar to Matthew. The two of them had the same sandy blonde hair, and even the same build. They could have been brothers, if not for the fact that they were from different countries.

"How lovely," Gwen said, clapping her hands together. "You all know me of course. I'm Gwen, and I inherited this bed and breakfast from my mother, who inherited it from *her* mother. Ewan?"

He waved. "I'm Ewan Ross. I've worked here seasonally for a few years now, and I help out doing odd jobs and anything Gwen or the guests need. I live just down the road, and I'm here almost every day, so if you need anything, just come and find me. I'll be going on the boat tour with you tomorrow as well. I've been on the thing a million times by now, so I'll be able to answer any questions you have that the captain doesn't have time to answer."

After that, they started eating. The food was home cooked and delicious, and the atmosphere was as peaceful and relaxed as she had hoped. She decided that she loved this little bed and breakfast, even though they hadn't been there for very long yet. Hopefully they would be able to come back one day, and maybe next time Violet and Marc could come along as well. She had a feeling their friends would love this place as well.

The sound of a barking dog woke Tulia up the next morning. She slipped out of bed and looked out the window to see a man throwing a bright orange toy into the water for the two dogs, who splashed in after it. She couldn't tell from this distance whether it was Christopher or Matthew, since they looked so similar. Then a horn sounded and she saw the man call the dogs back as a large boat pulled up along the rickety dock.

The tour wasn't supposed to leave until ten, so they still had a little time before they had to be ready, but she turned to wake Samuel up anyway. She wanted to make sure they had everything they needed for a day out on the water before they left.

Gwen sent them off with fresh bacon sandwiches and a thermos of coffee, along with the cooler that she had packed for lunch. The boat's captain introduced himself as Greg and welcomed the seven of them, including Ewan, on board. The dogs seemed eager to come along too, but Gwen held them back by their collars as they pulled away from the dock.

The loch was misty, giving the morning an ethereal feel as the shore slowly faded away behind them. Greg told them it would take about half an hour to cross to the fort, and told them to enjoy the cruise in the meantime. She and Samuel leaned against the railing, looking out over the misty waters together.

"It's a shame we didn't end up going to Loch Ness," he said. "It would have been fun to look for the Loch Ness monster."

"Well, maybe we'll get lucky and we'll be the first to discover the Loch Uiginn monster," Tulia said with a smile. "As long as it doesn't try to eat anyone, that is."

She heard laughter from further up the boat and turned to see the other guests standing at the prow, taking pictures of each other framed against the loch. Or, most them. She spotted Chloe and a man who at first she assumed to be her boyfriend standing on the other side of the cabin, kissing. But then the man turned his head and she realized it wasn't Ryan at all, but rather Matthew, who she could now tell apart from Christopher since he was dressed in snappier clothing than his doppelgänger.

She nudged Samuel, who turned to see what she had seen and raised an eyebrow.

"Somehow, I don't think her and Ryan's relation-ship is going to last very long," he murmured.

She shook her head. "I guess it's not any of our business, though."

He frowned, but slowly nodded. "I suppose you're right. We shouldn't get involved in other people's personal matters, especially not while we're on vacation."

As the sun rose, the mist began to fade, and before too long, she heard the splash of an anchor being dropped. The boat came to a stop not far from the far shore. She could see the ruins of an old fort rising out of the ground, and the entire group made their way over to the side of the boat to look at it. Greg stood at the prow, fiddling with a microphone attached to his shirt collar. The boat's speakers crackled.

"Can everyone hear me?" His voice came booming out of the speakers, and he winced and turned the volume down. "There, that's better. This is Fort Uiginn, which was built back in the 1400s. It was considered a highly defensible fort, and if you look over the opposite side of the boat, you'll see rocks just under the waves, which historians believe were put there on purpose to prevent an assault from across the loch. Unless you know the way through, chances are high that you would wreck your boat."

A couple of people moved to the other side of the boat to look in the water at the rocks.

"The fort was open to tours up until about five years ago when it fell into a state disrepair bad enough that the council closed it down until enough money is gathered for it to be made safe to enter again…"

He continued to talk about the history of the fort, and Tulia raised her cell phone to take a picture of the crumbling building. She was going to have a lot of material for her next blog post, which would include the announcement of her engagement. She didn't make much money from the blog, but it was a lot of fun to keep up with it.

Greg decided that they would stay there for lunch and eat near the fort. He stepped into the cabin to start arranging their meal while the others dispersed. Tulia and Samuel stayed at the railing, talking to each other about the fort and all of the history that had happened there.

"It's a shame we don't have anything like this in the US," she said. "I didn't fully realize how young our country was until we came to Europe. Everything here is so *old*."

"Yeah, we have a lot back home, but we're a little lacking when it comes to old castles," he murmured. "Before we go, it would be nice to –" He broke off at the sound of something large splashing into the water.

It sounded similar to when Greg had dropped the anchor in. Tulia turned around, wondering if there was a second anchor Greg had decided to drop down for some reason, but then she heard a scream.

"Someone went overboard!" Chloe shouted.

They all rushed over to the other side of the boat and peered down into the water. Tulia could see someone sinking slowly beneath the waves into the dark, almost black water of the loch. It was Matthew, she recognized his nice jacket billowing around him.

"Someone has to go help him," Samuel said. "He's not swimming."

Everyone else seemed to be frozen with shock, so he pulled off his boots and jumped over the railing. Tulia tightened her grip on the cold metal, watching as he dove underwater to lift the man up. Matthew was completely limp. Tulia looked around frantically and spotted a flotation device hanging on the side of the boat's cabin, which she grabbed off the boat and tossed down to him. He managed to get a grip on it, barely keeping the man's head above the water. Greg must have heard the commotion because he came out of the cabin and threw a rope down to Samuel, which Samuel tied under Matthew's arms. It took him and Greg working together to get Matthew back over the boat's railing.

"Oh my goodness," Chloe said as they laid him out on the deck. Ryan tightened his arms around her as she turned to hide her face. "He's not breathing."

Greg shooed them away and turned Matthew over to start CPR, but before he began, a frown creased his face. He withdrew his hand from the back of Matthew's head, and his fingers came away bloody.

"I don't think there's any helping him," he muttered. "This man's been killed."

CHAPTER THREE

Greg laid a tarp over Matthew's body, then wasted no time guiding the boat back across the loch to the bed and breakfast. Gwen was working outside in the garden, and looked up in surprise as the boat pulled up alongside the dock, hours early and full of silent guests.

"Is everything all right?" she called from the end of the dock as Ewan threw a rope to tie them down to the posts.

From the helm, Greg shook his head slowly. "Get a policeman out here, Gwen. There's been a death."

The woman's eyes widened, and she hurried back toward the bed and breakfast, calling the dogs with her.

Ewan secured the boat and swung open the gate,

allowing Tulia, Samuel, and the rest of the passengers to disembark. Greg followed them off onto the dock, then shut the gate behind him and stood with his arms crossed.

"I'll be waiting here until the police arrive," he said. "No one's to come onto the boat, you got it? If you left something behind, well, you can just wait for the authorities to get it for you."

Chloe sniffed and hurried away with Ryan's arm over her shoulders. Christopher paused, one thumb tucked around the strap of the ragged backpack he was wearing. "Do you think it was foul play?" he asked. "I didn't see what happened, but it seems to me like he could have just fallen overboard and hit his head on one of those rocks you were telling us about."

"I don't know what happened," Greg said. "But it's my boat and it's my responsibility. I don't want anyone interfering."

"I'll go make sure Gwen called this in," Ewan said. "Everyone else, it might be best if you return to your rooms. I'm sure the police will want to speak with everyone, so don't go driving off anywhere."

The six of them made their way back to the bed and breakfast. The dogs, as cheery as ever, greeted them at the door. Tulia patted their heads, enjoying their innocent happiness. She still wasn't able to tell them apart, but she figured the dogs didn't care as long as they got equal attention.

"Let's head up to our room," Samuel said. "We can talk up there."

She nodded, glancing at Ewan and Gwen, both of whom were standing behind the front desk. Gwen was on the phone, twisting the line around her finger as she talked to the police. Chloe and Ryan had already vanished down the hall. Christopher lingered by the door, then took a seat in the reading nook Matthew had been sitting in when Tulia and Samuel arrived the day before, looking uncertain. Tulia remembered that he was sleeping in the carriage house, and figured he probably wanted to be nearby when the police came.

With Matthew gone now, it was only her and Samuel upstairs. She waited until they got into their room to sigh, letting her purse drop onto the foot of the bed.

"I can't say this is how I wanted our vacation to end," she said. "I feel so bad for him. He was out there enjoying his first trip and things were finally looking up for him. It doesn't seem fair."

"I wish we had seen what happened," Samuel said as he sat down on the loveseat.

"I don't see why anyone would have pushed him off the boat," Tulia said. "No one here knows him well enough to have a grudge against him." She frowned. "Though, we did see him with Chloe. If Chloe's boyfriend found out she was cheating on him, maybe he had something to do with it."

"I suppose we'll have to get involved after all," Samuel said. "We'll have to tell the police what we saw, at least."

"I really hope this gets cleared up soon," she said. "It'll be difficult for the police to investigate, since some of us are from another country." She wrinkled her nose. "I suppose we'll be suspects too. It's probably very strange that this isn't the first time I've been a suspect in a possible homicide."

Despite everything, Samuel chuckled. "I suppose this is par for the course for us. Some things never change, do they?"

The police arrived just a few minutes later. No one came up to fetch Tulia and Samuel, so they watched out the window as the police milled around the boat and the dock. Someone backed an ambulance up, and she could see them removing Matthew's body from the boat.

As she watched, one of the officers left the boat with an opaque evidence bag in his hands. It was large, and she wondered what was inside of it. She couldn't think of what might have been left behind on the boat that could be considered evidence. Unless the boat had video cameras she hadn't noticed? She hadn't exactly been looking for them while she was enjoying the tour.

It wasn't until after the ambulance left that Ewan came up to knock on their door and tell them the police were ready to talk to everyone.

When they got downstairs, an officer told her they were questioning everyone one by one in the dining room. She and Samuel went in separately. They called him first, and he squeezed her hand when he came out, gesturing for her to go inside. She sat across the dining table from the detective, who was a man in his fifties with graying hair. He gave her a kind smile and started off by asking her a little about herself. Despite his accent, he was easy enough to talk to, and she didn't have anything to hide anyway, so she wasn't very nervous. After asking her a little about her reasons for taking this trip and where else they had gone, he finally got down to the point.

"I'd like you to tell me everything you can remember about your boat trip on the loch," he said gently. "Even if it seems unimportant."

She did as he asked, giving him an overview of everything she had seen and heard on the boat. She even told him about seeing Chloe with Matthew just an hour or so before his death.

"Her boyfriend, Ryan, was on the other side of the boat, taking pictures with the others," she said. "I don't know if he knew what was going on, and Samuel and I didn't say anything to him, but that's the only incident that really stands out to me. Samuel and I were looking at the fort when we heard the scream. Matthew fell off on the other side of the boat, opposite the shore."

"Was he the one who screamed?"

She shook her head. "No. Chloe was the one who screamed. She was the only other woman on the boat besides me, and it was definitely a woman who screamed. She's the one who shouted that someone had fallen into the water, too. I don't know if she saw what happened – we didn't talk much with the other guests on the way back. Everyone was a little shocked, I think."

"Most people would be, in that situation. Thank you for taking the time to talk to me. I just want to assure you that you're not a suspect, but I *am* going to ask if you can stay in the area for little while, while we look into this. You mentioned your vacation was almost over. When were you planning on going home?"

"Our flight leaves Monday afternoon. I think we're planning on leaving the bed and breakfast early in the morning. Our flight is out of Glasgow. Do we need to delay it?"

He shook his head. "No, no, nothing like that. If we need to talk to you again, I'll make sure we do it before Monday. But there shouldn't be any problems. If you do end up needing to leave sooner than that, can you just call down to the station and let us know?"

"Of course," she said.

"Well, that's it, I think. You're the last one I had to talk to. We'll be heading off now, though I expect the station will send someone out in the morning to pick up Matthew's belongings. We'll want to get those back to his family in the states, even if this investigation doesn't go anywhere. Stay safe, all right? I hope you're able to salvage the rest of your vacation. This is a terrible tragedy, but so far every-one's handled it exactly as they should have. I'll be giving Gwen a call once we know where we're going with this case. If you're still around, I'm sure she'll update you."

She shook his hand and they left the dining area together. It had been a surprisingly laid-back ques-tioning, but she was still glad to rejoin Samuel and the others, who were all gathered around the front desk, while Gwen chatted with one of the younger officers, who she seemed to know.

It made her realize that this really was a small, rural area. The closest town was a tiny village. These people were a community, and she, Samuel, and the others were all outsiders.

She was just glad the police didn't seem to be too hostile toward them. It was a little intimidating to be involved with a major legal issue like this in another country, but it could have gone worse.

CHAPTER FOUR

After the police left, Tulia and Samuel returned to their room. She started working on her next blog post while he typed out an email to Marc to tell him what was going on. With the window cracked open and the fresh air from the lake coming in, it made for a peaceful break. As afternoon began to turn into evening, they decided to swing by the village and pick up some snacks and souvenirs. They passed by Gwen folding laundry in the reading nook, and she waved them down before they could leave.

"Are the two of you heading out?"

"We thought we'd go down to the village," Samuel said. "Is that going to be an issue? The police just told us we had to stay in the area."

"Oh, no, it's perfectly fine. I hate to ask, but I was wondering if you could pick up some takeout for everyone while you're there. I've been so distracted by everything that happened this morning I haven't even gotten started on dinner. I was going to send Ewan off, but he asked to leave early. I can't say I blame him, so I told him he could have the rest of the day off. Christopher doesn't have a car, of course, or I'd send him instead. I was just about to leave myself, but if you don't mind, it would make things a little easier for me for you to pick it up."

"We don't mind at all," Tulia said. "What do you want us to get?"

Gwen went over to the phone on the front desk and called one of her favorite restaurants in town to place an order big enough to feed all of them, then handed over a wad of foreign bills.

"Just bring back the change. Thanks, you two. I do appreciate it."

Tulia sorted through the money while Samuel drove them to the village. Even after weeks in Europe, she was fascinated by the foreign currency. Paying with it was self-explanatory, of course, but it still felt so strange to pay with something other than American dollars.

She found a few cute souvenirs in town, which she bought up guilt-free. She already had half a suitcase full of the things from the various countries they had been to, but she could afford the extra baggage fees. The airlines charged an arm and a leg for checked bags, but there were certain benefits to having won the lottery.

They unloaded the bags of takeout in the dining room when they got back to the bed and breakfast. Gwen told them they were welcome to dine in there with her, or they could take their food back to their rooms if they needed time to process the morning's events. Then she went off to get the others. Ryan was the only one who came out of his and Chloe's room, and he gathered up enough food for both of them.

"Chloe's still pretty upset," he said as they watched him take the food. "We're going to eat in our room together." He sighed. "I don't know why that man's death hit her so hard. She's not usually so sensitive."

"She did just witness someone die," Tulia said, feeling like she had to defend the other woman despite the fact that she had been cheating on her boyfriend. She didn't think being upset at witnessing someone's last moments of life meant she was being too sensitive. Something about the way Ryan said it rubbed her the wrong way.

"Yeah, I guess," Ryan muttered. "It just isn't how I wanted to spend the trip, you know?"

With a sigh, he carried the food out of the dining room. Christopher poked his head in a few moments later and seemed to silently debate with himself whether he wanted to eat there or take his meal back to the carriage house, but Gwen waved him in and had him sit down. The dogs tried to follow them, but she got up to shoo them away and shut the door.

"They're terrible about begging for food," she explained. "You're going to sit with us, mister. I still have to find a way to put you to work. Do you mind doing the dishes after dinner?"

"I can do that," he said, taking the food. "Thanks again for letting me stay for so cheap."

She waved him off, offering him a weak smile. "Oh, it's perfectly fine. We get plenty of backpackers up here, and I know the village doesn't have a hostel. You aren't going to be staying for free, though, so don't you take off without putting in your fair share of labor. I've got a bunch of firewood that needs chopped, maybe you can do that tomorrow."

He grimaced but didn't complain as he started eating. Tulia and Samuel served themselves plates and settled in for a peaceful, if quiet, meal before returning upstairs for the evening.

They called it an early night, wanting to get an early start at getting back to being tourists tomorrow. When Tulia opened her eyes in the middle of the night, she wasn't sure at first what had woken her. She had left the window cracked open, and she could hear the crickets outside, but that was too soothing to have woken her.

Then she heard a thud come from the room next door. She turned over in the bed, mentally dismissing it as another guest, but then she froze and her heart rate ratcheted up.

Matthew had been the one in the room next to theirs. Unless he had returned as an angry ghost, there shouldn't be anyone in that room right now. During the day, she might have put up to Gwen or Ewan cleaning, but there was no way either of them was cleaning in there in the middle of the night.

She heard the sound of something thumping against the wall, then a moment later, she heard a door shut. She forced herself into action, nudging Samuel until he woke up.

"What is it?" he asked sleepily.

"I heard something next door," she whispered. "In Matthew's room."

It took a second for him to make the connection, but when he did, he sat up quickly.

"No one should be over there."

"I know," she hissed. "What should we do?"

"I'll go see what's going on," he said. "Stay behind me."

She stayed close to his back as he strode across the room and opened the door, stepping out into the hall. She inched into the hallway beside him and looked over at Matthew's door. It was shut tightly, but she knew what she had heard. Samuel raised his hand to knock on the door, but there was no answer. After a moment, he turned the doorknob and pushed it open. It wasn't locked, which didn't tell her much. It was so peaceful out here, Matthew might have thought it was safe to leave it unlocked while they were on the loch.

Samuel let out a low whistle when he saw the interior of the room. Tulia peeked around him and bit her lip at the sight. It had been ransacked. The drawers had been pulled open, the bed stripped of its bedding. It looked like everything of value was gone. The only belongings of Matthew's she could see were a few items of clothing strewn about.

"We've got to go get Gwen," Samuel said.

Still in their pajamas, they went downstairs, only to realize they didn't actually know where Gwen slept. They had a rough idea of where Chloe and Ryan's room was, and they knew Christopher was sleeping in the carriage house, so it just took a little looking around before they found a promising door. Tulia knocked on it, thinking Gwen might prefer to be woken up in the middle of the night by a strange woman then a strange man.

She had to knock twice before the door opened. Gwen was wearing an old-fashioned nightgown and squinted out at them, looking like she had just woken up. One of the dogs stared up at them from her side, wagging her fluffy golden tail in welcome.

"Is there a problem?"

"I woke up hearing sounds in Matthew's room, which is right next to ours," Tulia explained. "We checked, and whoever was in there is gone, but the room has been completely ransacked."

Gwen's eyes widened.

"Thank you for letting me know. I'm going to get some proper clothes on, then I'll take a peek at it and round everyone else up to see if anyone else saw anything. I really hope this was just a nasty prank by one of the other guests, and not something more serious."

Tulia and Samuel returned to the common area to wait while Gwen got changed. No one else seemed to be up. The bed and breakfast was all but silent. She hoped Gwen was right, and this was some sort of strange misunderstanding or prank, but she doubted it. Whoever had taken Matthew's things had to know that the man was dead. Was the thief just an opportunist, or had they killed Matthew?

CHAPTER FIVE

Gwen woke the other guests up and brought Christopher in from the carriage house. They all gathered in the common area, and Gwen notified them that she was going to be checking each of their rooms for the missing items.

"I won't be going through anyone's bags or personal belongings," she assured them, cutting off their complaints. "I'm just going to be taking a quick look around. I peeked at Matthew's room, and a lot has been taken. I don't think anyone here would have had time to hide it all away yet. If anyone wants to come with me and watch, they are welcome to. I hate feeling like I'm blaming any of my guests for this, but theft is a crime, and not only that, but all of those items might become a part of the investigation into Matthew's death."

Chloe and Ryan didn't look happy. Christopher just looked tired. He had his ragged backpack with him, and raised a hand to get Gwen's attention.

"Do you need to look through this?"

She shook her head. "No, no. Unless you somehow managed to fit a few full-sized suitcases in there, I think you're in the clear. Like I said, I'm just going to take a peek into your rooms, and I suppose your rental cars too." She gave Tulia and Samuel a grimace in apology. Tulia guessed that Gwen didn't really consider them suspects, since they had been the ones to notify her of the theft, but she probably didn't want to show any favoritism toward them. Tulia gave her a reassuring smile. She didn't mind the older woman poking her head into their room or looking through their rental car at all, and probably would have done the same thing in her position.

They all waited in the common room, except for Ryan, who went with Gwen when she looked through his and Chloe's guest room. It didn't take the older woman long to inspect the property. When she came in from the carriage house, she looked a little more cheerful.

"Well, that's a relief. I'm glad none of you did it, but of course that means we had someone else come in from outside of the bed and breakfast. It's quite concerning. I'm guessing it was someone from the village who heard about Matthew's death and decided to make some money pawning his things before anyone thought to look for them. I'm going to ring up the police in the morning. I don't think this is worth calling the emergency line for. We should be safe here tonight, but I suggest all of you lock your doors. I'm going to leave Heather and Honey out and about in the main area instead of bringing them into my room. Hopefully, they'll bark if someone comes by again. I'm going to make a quick pot of tea to calm my nerves, so if anyone wants some, just let me know."

It took a while to fall back to sleep after that, but when she did, Tulia slept through the rest of the night without any further disturbances.

Gwen hadn't said anything about breakfast, and as far as Tulia knew, dinner was the only meal included in their stay. The other woman had sent them off with breakfast sandwiches the day of the boat tour, but she thought that was a special thing. She and Samuel decided to go into town to grab breakfast, but first, Tulia had to make a video call.

She propped up her laptop on the table in front of the loveseat and turned on the screen, smiling as Violet's face came into view. Cicero, her African gray parrot, was perched on her shoulder.

"Say hi," Violet said to the bird. "Look, there she is."

Cicero tilted his head to one side and let out a sharp whistle, which crackled as it came over the laptop speakers. Tulia smiled and waved at her bird.

"Hey, buddy. How's it going? I miss you."

He bobbed his head up and down as Violet said, "Everything's been going well here. Marc told me all about what happened at that bed and breakfast the two of you are staying at. I hope everything's okay."

"Well, something interesting happened last night…"

She told Violet about the theft in Matthew's room. Her friend looked concerned. "I hope you're being careful. Maybe you should come back early."

Tulia grimaced. "I really don't want to have to do that. But we'll see how things turn out."

"As long as you're safe," Violet said with a yawn. "I'm going to let you go now. It's late here. I'll call again this weekend. I hope you two enjoy the rest of your vacation."

Samuel sat down next to her to say goodbye to Violet, then Tulia shut the laptop.

"Well, I'm glad they're still doing well," she said. "Are you ready to get going?"

"I am," he said. "Let's go see what breakfast foods this little village has to offer."

They went downstairs, where they found Chloe and Ryan deep in a discussion by the front door. The two of them fell silent as Tulia and Samuel approached. Chloe shot her boyfriend a sharp glare and he sighed before saying, "We were just talking about inviting you two to go get breakfast with us. Were you about to go to the village?"

"We are," Tulia said. "But we don't want to intrude." He didn't seem thrilled with the idea.

"No, it's fine. Besides, the village probably only has one or two restaurants open this early. It would just be awkward if we ended up at the same place and tried to ignore each other the whole time."

"That's not all," Chloe said. "There's something we want to talk to you about."

Tulia exchanged an intrigued look with Samuel. "Well, we're happy to join you."

Chloe nodded, looking pleased. "Great. I'm going to go ask Christopher."

She slipped out the front door and the rest of them

followed her. Outside, Tulia could hear the sharp sound of someone chopping wood. They walked around the corner of the bed and breakfast, into a small yard between it and the old carriage house. Tulia still hadn't seen the interior. She suspected it was done up as a sort of hostel – she couldn't imagine Christopher had been sleeping on a pile of straw this whole time. He was busy chopping wood with an axe, but paused when he saw them, resting the axe on his shoulder.

"Hi," Chloe said. "We're going into town for breakfast. Do you want to join us?"

He shook his head. "Thanks, but I ate already. Gwen made me a fried egg sandwich before she sent me out here to work. I've got to get this done, since I did promise I would do some labor for her in exchange for staying here."

"All right, well if you change your mind, we'll just be in the village," Chloe said.

Tulia and Samuel followed Ryan and Chloe into the nearby village, where they pulled up in front of the one restaurant that was open this early. Nearly half the tables were filled with locals when they went inside, and there was a sign up telling them to seat themselves, so they took a booth in the back corner. Tulia looked over the menu and decided to order the traditional Scottish breakfast, which was a lot like the English breakfast she had tried back in London, but with the addition of potato scones, some sort of flat sausage, and something called white pudding, which unlike black pudding, wasn't made out of blood. It seemed promising already.

After they ordered, Chloe broached the topic she wanted to discuss with them. "Okay, now that we're out of there, I can say what we've all been thinking. Ewan is super suspicious, isn't he?"

Beside her, Ryan sighed. Samuel raised his eyebrows. Tulia just blinked. The local, seasonal worker at the bed and breakfast wasn't exactly the sort of person she would call suspicious. He seemed perfectly normal to her.

"You'll need to clarify that," Samuel said.

"I told her she is out of her mind," Ryan complained.

"Oh, hush," Chloe snapped at him. "Just hear me out. So, we know he left early last night. The thing is, I saw Gwen lock the front door before we all went to bed. If someone broke in and stole all of Matthew's things, it has to have been someone with a key. It also makes sense that the dogs wouldn't have barked when he came into the bed and breakfast, since they're so familiar with him. Plus, he knew that the police were coming back for Matthew's things in the morning, and he's also the only one who Gwen didn't question about the missing items. What I think happened is, he came back to the bed and breakfast in the middle of the night, used his key to get in, moved all of Matthew's things out, and went home before Gwen even woke up. Since he left early the night before, it makes sense that she wouldn't consider him a suspect. I'm not saying he murdered Matthew or anything – I still think that was probably just an accident. As far as the theft goes though, I'm pretty much certain it was Ewan."

"That's not a bad theory," Tulia said. "But since none of us saw anything, it would be hard to prove."

"He said he lives just up the road, right?" Chloe asked. "We could go to his house and snoop around. He was already at the bed and breakfast when I woke up this morning – I think he's supposed to be helping Christopher with the firewood, so we know he'll be there for a while. If we don't do it, he might never get found out. This is such a… quaint little village, the police might be reluctant to investigate a local, especially since the victim is already dead and there's not really anyone who is going to be pressuring them to work on the case."

"I don't think it's fair to imply that the police

wouldn't do their jobs," Samuel said. "And I definitely don't think it's a good idea to trespass on someone's property, especially when we are all foreigners. I'm not saying your theory isn't solid, but you might be better off just having a chat with the local police and letting it go."

"I told her it was a stupid plan," Ryan said. "Sorry for wasting your time like this."

"It's not waste of time," Tulia said. "We're still going to get some good food out of it, after all, and I do think she has a point. But I'm with Samuel on this – I'm not about to bend or break any laws when I'm in a foreign country. That seems like a recipe for disaster."

Chloe wilted. "Yeah. I guess I didn't think of it like that. I just… It bothers me so much that he's probably going to get away with this. Everything that happened to Matthew was so unfair."

Ryan heaved another sigh. "You barely knew the guy. We met him, like, two days before he died. Can't you just let it go?"

The two of them started squabbling, but broke off when the server arrived with their food. Tulia picked up her fork, eager to try the local breakfast. She didn't know whether Chloe was right or wrong, and she still didn't have a high opinion of the woman after she saw her kissing Matthew on the boat, but she wasn't Ryan's biggest fan either. He seemed very dismissive of everything his girlfriend said. She wouldn't miss either of them when it was time for her and Samuel to go back home.

CHAPTER SIX

"That was good," Chloe said when they finished. "Though I miss all of the variety we have at home. We have five different all-night restaurants in a five minute walk from our apartment. It will be good to get back."

"Can't you just enjoy the trip?" Ryan said. "When we were back home in California, you were always complaining about how we never went anywhere or did anything, and now that we're in the UK, it's like you can hardly wait to get home."

Chloe's face twisted. "I *have* been having a good time. Well, up until that poor man died. I'm just saying it will be nice to get home too."

"Tulia and I feel the same way," Samuel told her. "We've been gone for a couple weeks now, and while it has been an amazing trip, it will be great to get home to our friends and have things get back to normal."

Chloe shot him a brief, grateful smile. "What do the two of you have planned for today?"

Tulia and Samuel glanced at each other and shrugged. "We don't have any specific plans," Tulia said. "We'll probably explore the area a bit."

"I was thinking we could find somewhere nice to hike," Samuel said. "It seems like it's going to be a good day for it."

"Oh, Ryan, we should go hiking too," Chloe said, nudging her boyfriend. "It would be nice to spend a day out in nature, and the views around here are so beautiful."

He shrugged. "Sure, sounds all right to me. I guess we'll see if the bed and breakfast has a guide to the local paths or something."

They paid for their meal and headed back toward the bed and breakfast. Tulia and Samuel parked in their old spot and got out of the car. Christopher was pacing back and forth in front of the door, talking to someone on his cell phone. When he saw them and a second later, Chloe and Ryan, getting out of their vehicles, he ended the call and slipped the phone into his pocket.

"How was breakfast? Did you find a good place to eat?"

"It was nice," Tulia said. "The food was all freshly cooked, and delicious. Are you done chopping wood?"

"Yep, I got it all done. I think I'm going to head into town pretty soon. Do you remember seeing a library or some sort of internet café? I need better Wi-Fi than this place has."

"I don't think I saw anything like that, but I wasn't looking for it," Tulia said.

"I'll ask Gwen," he said.

Chloe and Ryan reached them, and all of them went into the bed and breakfast. Ewan was polishing the front desk with a spray that smelled like oranges, but gave them a brief smile when they came in.

"Welcome back. Dinner is going to be fish and chips, so if you don't like fish, you'd better let Gwen know."

"We were wondering if you have any maps of the local walking paths," Chloe said as Gwen came around the corner with a basket of fresh laundry. "The four of us were thinking of going on a hike."

Tulia wasn't certain they had actually agreed to go together, but it would be rude to say anything against it now.

Gwen brightened up instantly when she heard what Chloe said. She put the laundry basket down and said, "Ewan knows all of the best areas to go for a walk." She turned to him. "Why don't you go with them and show them that lovely little lake not far from here? You'll be hiking a distance around the loch, so I'll whip up a picnic for you to take before you go."

Ewan hesitated. "I have a lot to do around here. I was going to sweep, and then finish the dishes in the kitchen –"

"Oh, I can do all of that," Gwen said. "You should go off and have some fun. It's a lovely day. We're supposed to get rain tomorrow, so you might as well enjoy it while you can. Besides, we wouldn't want our guests getting lost. Let me see, how many sandwiches do I need to make?"

She started counting them, but when she reached Christopher, he shook his head. "Thanks, but I need to go into town. I need to get online, and the internet here just isn't cutting it."

"Hold on just a second and I'll give you directions to the library," she told him. "Five sandwiches it is, then. I'll pack you some juice as well, and a bit of fruit. Give me just a few minutes."

She bustled away. Ewan looked a little irritated

that he was being strong-armed into a hike when it seemed like he had his day already planned, but didn't say anything about it. Tulia had been hoping for some time alone with Samuel, but she felt like there was no backing out now, and by the look on Samuel's face, he agreed. She decided to make the best of it. It would still be a nice hike, and at least this way, they wouldn't have to worry about getting lost. And even if someone here *was* responsible for Matthew's death or the theft of his belongings, there would be safety in numbers. In fact, maybe going as a group was best after all.

Gwen came back a few minutes later with a wicker picnic basket and a folded blanket. She handed the supplies to Ewan, then passed a piece of paper over to Christopher. "These are the directions to the library. It should be about a ten minute walk from here. If they give you any trouble about not having a card, just give them my name. They can ring me up here and I'll let them know you're a guest. I doubt they'll let you check out any books, but you should be able to use their computers."

"Do they have Wi-Fi? That's what I really need. I'd like to use my own computer for this."

"Yes, yes, that should be fine," Gwen said distractedly. "Go on now, Ewan. You five have a nice time. I'll get started on dinner in a couple of hours, so you'll have a warm meal waiting for you shortly after you get back."

Ewan sighed and turned toward the door. "Come on, let's go. It'll be a bit of a walk, but I'm sure you'll appreciate the view."

He held the door open and they all headed out. Tulia watched as Christopher walked the opposite direction from the rest of them, heading toward the village. She wondered what he needed to get online so urgently for, but it wasn't any of her business. He had said he was trying to figure out what he wanted to do with his life — maybe it had something to do with that.

She felt a little bad about how quickly everyone was moving on from Matthew's death, though none of them had known him very well. She guessed that the police had already come and gone to take a report about his missing items while they were at breakfast. She just hoped the matter was resolved quickly. Matthew's family deserved to have his belongings back, even if he would never be going home.

CHAPTER SEVEN

Ewan led them around the bed and breakfast to a path that bordered the loch. It wasn't a hard hike, though they had a few hills to climb. The land was a lot more open than a lot of the places Tulia had gone hiking. This was nothing like the Pacific Northwest, where she had gone on what had become her most recent memorable hike, but it was beautiful in its own way.

It wasn't supposed to rain, but the sky grew slightly overcast as they walked. After what she estimated to be about a mile, the path took a turn away from the loch, leading further inland. They passed a field with sheep in it, and the woolly creatures raised their heads to watch them go by. Finally, they crested a hill and Ewan paused.

"Here it is."

It was a small lake, bordered by willows on one edge, with a large rock protruding from the deepest part of the lake.

"In the summer, kids like to swim here and jump off that rock," he told them. "Even in the fall, it's a nice place for a picnic. Why don't you all walk around a bit, and I'll get the food set up."

Samuel took Tulia's hand, and they walked down to the lake together. It was unbelievably peaceful out here. She knew they weren't very far from the village, but with the hills blocking their view of civilization, it felt extremely rural.

"I love living in Loon Bay," she said. "But it would be amazing to live somewhere like this one day, too."

"Maybe one day," he said. "Once the PI business has been doing well for a few years, we can look into moving, or maybe even expanding into a different state entirely."

She smiled at him warmly. She had her own apartment right now, but the lease was going to be up in just a few months. She felt another thrill at the thought that they were actually engaged. She and Samuel had to start planning for the future together, because they were going to be a team from here on out.

Chloe and Ryan went off on their own walk around the lake, though they came back as Ewan was putting the finishing touches on the picnic. They all sat down on the blanket together, and Ewan reached for the picnic basket.

"What are you doing with that?" Chloe snapped, making Tulia jump. Her eyes were on Ewan. He pulled his hand away from the basket and gave her a confused look.

"I was just going to take the sandwiches out."

"No, you know that's not what I'm talking about. That watch. Where did you get it?"

He tugged the left sleeve of his shirt down over his wrist. Tulia caught a glint of a golden watchband before it was covered.

"I've had this for years," he muttered, crossing his arms and effectively hiding it from view. "What are you on about?"

"That's Matthew's watch," Chloe said. "I would know it anywhere. He told me all about it. He was super proud of it."

"How would you know that, Chloe?" Ryan snapped, glaring at his girlfriend. "We stayed at the same bed and breakfast as the guy for two days. You've been acting like your best friend died or something. When would he even have had time to tell you about some special watch he had?"

Chloe flushed and looked away from him. "Just trust me, I know it's his watch. Ewan stole it. He's the one who took everything out of Matthew's room, just like I said earlier."

"Hold on," Ewan said. "When were you talking about me?"

"Seriously, Chloe, what's going on? Was there something between you and that Matthew guy?" Ryan asked, ignoring Ewan. Chloe wouldn't meet his gaze, and his eyes widened slightly. "There was! Enough of this, Chloe. Just tell me the truth."

"It – it wasn't what you think. It wasn't anything serious," she said, her voice breaking. "I ran into him when I left the room to get extra towels that first night, and we chatted a little and realized how much we have in common... Nothing happened, I swear."

"I don't believe that. You've been going on about him ever since he died. Tell me the truth, or I'm leaving right now. You can find your own way back home."

"No, Ryan," she said, grasping his arm with both her hands. "We only kissed, I swear. That's it."

He pulled away from her. "I thought you said nothing happened? A kiss isn't nothing. This is ridiculous." He stood up, and Chloe rose too, reaching for him again. He pushed her away.

"I think that's enough," Samuel said, rising to his feet. Tulia mirrored him, sparing a sad glance for the forgotten picnic basket. "It's not a good idea to get physical with each other. I think we should all head back to the bed and breakfast and you two can figure this out there."

"Yeah, I'm done here," Ryan said. He started stomping back toward the bed and breakfast. Chloe followed him for a few steps, then stopped and started crying, burying her face in her hands.

Slowly, Ewan started folding up the picnic blanket.

The hike back to the bed and breakfast was mostly silent. Ryan stayed ahead of them, and Chloe stumbled along behind him, looking lost, while Ewan trailed along at the back of the group. When the bed and breakfast finally came into view, Ryan stomped through the door without waiting for them. By the time the rest of them got inside, he was already talking to Gwen.

"I don't care if it's going to cost more, I want my own room. Chloe and I are done."

"Ryan, please, just give me a chance to make it up to you," she begged.

"No. It's over. If you're willing to cheat on me with some guy you've known for a few hours when we're on a trip in another country together, I don't want to know what the rest of my life with you would be like. This isn't up for debate. I'm going to get my stuff out of the room, and then I don't want to talk to you again."

Gwen looked pale, her gaze flitting between the two of them. "Of course, I can give you separate rooms. Just give me a second to get another one tidied up for you. Ewan?"

"Yeah, I'll go do it. I'll do the one upstairs, across the hall from where Matthew was staying." He started walking away, but Chloe called out again.

"Wait! We still have to talk about the watch. Show it to us."

He paused and raised his left hand and pulling the shirtsleeve down. A silver watch on a black band stood out on his wrist. Tulia frowned. She was certain it had been gold before.

"It's my watch. My father gave it to me when I turned eighteen."

"He's right," Gwen said. "He's had that watch ever since he started working for me."

Chloe looked confused and lost, and Ewan headed upstairs without another word. Tulia nudged Samuel and nodded toward the stairs. They could let Gwen deal with figuring out Ryan and Chloe's relationship problems if they started arguing again. She and Samuel went upstairs and into their own room, shutting the door on the sounds of Ewan tidying up the new room for Ryan.

"I'm not going crazy, right?" she asked, keeping her voice low. "The watch he had on before was gold with a gold band."

"I saw the same thing," Samuel murmured. "Something's going on here."

CHAPTER EIGHT

"I think we should try to get to the bottom of this," Samuel said. They were sitting together on the loveseat, and had been debating the pros and cons of getting involved. "I know we can't do much, we aren't even in the United States and there is no way my private investigator's license is good here, but as long as we stay in the realm of legality, I think it will be okay."

"Well, the first thing we should try to figure out is what happened to that other watch he was wearing," Tulia said. "He wouldn't have had time to hide it after we got back to the bed and breakfast. He was standing right there the whole time."

"I doubt he had it on him," Samuel mused. "If one

of us pushed the issue and asked him to empty out his pockets, it would be too risky."

"So he must've dropped it somewhere," she concluded. "While we were hiking back, I mean. It could be anywhere between here and the lake."

"Well, are you up for another walk? With him busy setting up the room for Ryan, he's not going to have time to get out there and find it for a while. If we're going to go, we should do it now."

She rose from the loveseat. "Yeah, let's head out. The path seemed pretty straightforward, so we shouldn't get lost."

They put their shoes back on and then returned to the bottom floor of the bed and breakfast after checking to make sure Ewan was still working on getting the room ready for Ryan. Chloe was nowhere to be seen, Christopher was still gone, and Gwen was somewhere else in the building. No one was there to ask them what they were doing as they left.

They walked around to the back and found the little path along the loch. They moved slowly, keeping their eyes on the path and the tall grass that bordered it on either side. Even so, Tulia almost missed it. She thought she spotted a glint of gold and backtracked, peering into the weeds. And there, she saw it. A gold wristwatch, sitting off to the side of the path. It was tucked in a clump of nettles, and was only visible because the sun had come back out and the sunlight was glinting off of the golden band.

She stooped and picked it up carefully. Samuel looked at it, then met her eyes.

"We weren't seeing things."

She shook her head. "We still don't have any proof this was Matthew's watch, though."

"Is there anything inscribed on it?"

She turned it over, looking at the back of the watch. There were initials carved onto the back plate. BRJ.

"Well, that J could be Jameson, but Matthew definitely doesn't have a name that starts with the letter B. Maybe it was an heirloom from a family member?"

"Maybe," he said. "We really don't know that much about him. I wonder if he has much of a presence online."

"We can check," she said. She slipped it into her purse, wishing she had thought to bring a plastic bag for it. They headed back toward the bed and breakfast, the walk feeling a lot shorter now that they weren't looking through the weeds and grass. When they arrived, she was surprised to see another car in the parking lot. It was backed up to the carriage house. Christopher must have heard their footsteps, because he came out of the carriage house and waved at them.

"How is your hike?" he asked, sounding cheerful.

"It could have been better," she called out. "Did you get what you needed at the library?"

"I did. I'll have to thank Gwen. I took a bus to the bigger town about ten miles away and got a rental car, too. I think I'm going to head off in the morning. There's no real reason for me to stay longer, especially with everything that's been going on here. It's not much of a vacation anymore."

"Didn't the police say to stay in the area?" Samuel asked.

Christopher shrugged. "Well, they haven't come back to talk to any of us. I'll swing by the station on my way out of town to let them know I'm leaving, I guess. Have you seen the inside of the carriage house yet? It's actually pretty nice, I'm really grateful Gwen let me stay here even when I couldn't pay her."

Tulia shook her head and he stepped back, opening the door for them to enter. The interior was comfortable, with patterned wallpaper on the drywall and a series of bunks along the walls. There was a bathroom off to one side, and a small TV hung on one of the walls.

"It's basically a small hostel," he said. "She allows people who can't afford to stay in the guest-house to stay here in exchange for work. It seems to work out pretty well for her. I do still owe her a little, so I'm going to see if I can pay that off before I leave."

"This is a nice set up," Tulia said as they left the carriage hour, the three of them heading toward the bed and breakfast. "She must have a great life out here. I'm so jealous she gets to live somewhere like this."

Christopher laughed. "It *is* nice, but I think most people would go stir crazy out here. Nothing ever happens in these small villages. I've never understood why people are so content to stay in the same place their whole lives."

"I guess not everyone can afford to travel," she said. "Or has the urge to. I didn't really travel anywhere until I turned thirty. She does seem happy, though. Everyone's different, so I'm not going to judge her for it. I can see the allure of a life like this, though I do think it would get boring after a while."

Christopher strode ahead to open the door for the two of them, and she and Samuel went inside. She didn't see any reason to bring the pocket watch up to him, but she did want to tell Gwen about it. She wasn't sure where to find the other woman, though, and it was Ewan who appeared from down the hall when he heard them come in.

"Do you folks need anything?" he asked. "I was just about to head out again. I might be gone for about an hour."

"I don't think so," Samuel said. "Do you know if Gwen is around?"

He shook his head. "She ran into town to get some supplies for dinner. She should be back in fifteen or twenty minutes. I'm going on break, so you'll need to wait until then if you need anything."

He nodded to them and left, shutting the door behind him. Tulia exchanged a look with Samuel. Was he going to look for the wristwatch he had discarded earlier? It seemed to be burning a hole in her purse. She really wanted to tell Gwen about it and then contact the police, but it sounded like it was going to have to wait.

"I'm going to grab some fresh towels and take a shower, since it sounds like Gwen isn't around," Christopher said. "I'll see the two of you at dinner."

He gave them a jaunty wave as they started toward the stairs. Tulia waved back, a little bemused. He hadn't been unpleasant exactly, but he had certainly been on the quieter side during the earlier part of their stay. Something seemed to have put him in a good mood. Maybe it was just the fact that he had a rental car now, and wouldn't have to walk or ride a bus to wherever he was going next.

Once they were in their room, Samuel shut the door and they both sat back down on the loveseat. She took the wristwatch out of her purse and put it on the table in front of them.

"Now what?" she asked.

He nodded at her laptop. "Now, we put our detective skills to work. Maybe we should have gone to the police straightaway, but it seems polite to talk to Gwen first since she's his employer and this is her property – and we still don't have any proof it belonged to Matthew. We can wait a few minutes until she gets back, and there's no harm in trying to figure out whose initials these are. Some proof it belonged to him will strengthen our case when we go to the police."

She nodded and opened her laptop, typing in the password before going to her social media account. She didn't use it much anymore, not since she had won the lottery and started her blog, but it had come in useful quite a few times for tracking down information on suspects and victims alike.

"All right, he said he was from New York State,

right? His name is pretty common, so might take a while to find him, but if we can narrow down, that should help." She typed his name into the search bar and hit enter.

It was time to find out who Matthew Jameson really was, and see if they could tie the wristwatch they had found to him.

CHAPTER NINE

It took a while to find the right Matthew Jameson online. Between New York state being such a populated region and the name being a relatively common one, even by narrowing it down to people who didn't live in New York City itself, there were a lot of results to go through.

Finally, they found a profile with a picture that showed Matthew standing in front of a beach, smiling. Tulia felt a pang as she clicked on it. It didn't look like he posted a lot. The last public post she could see was a cheerful announcement that he was leaving on his trip to the UK, and would be back in a couple of weeks.

There was nothing after that. It seemed as if his

family hadn't made any posts about his death. It had only been a few days – she couldn't blame them for wanting to keep it private for the time being.

She scrolled through his friend list, but didn't see anyone with the initials BRJ.

"We could try to ask one of his family members about it," Samuel suggested. "We don't need to get into the details yet, not until we know what's going on, but we could say we found the watch and wanted to see if it was his."

"Who do we ask, though?" she said. "I don't want to bother his mother or his sister with something like this. They've got enough on their plates, dealing with his loss. It wouldn't be fair to them."

"Maybe not an immediate family member? See if you can find someone who's listed as an extended family member and who seems to be online a lot."

She scrolled through his profile some more until she noticed that a woman by the name of Catherine Tanis not only replied to a lot of his posts with vague, upbeat messages, but was also listed as his aunt on his profile. The woman seemed to be online a lot, and seemed involved in her nephew's life, even though her profile said she lived in California. She seemed like a good candidate – she would likely know if he had an heirloom watch, but probably wouldn't be quite as devastated by his death as his more immediate family members were.

"All right, I'm going to message her," she said. "I'm not sure when she'll see it, since there is such a big time difference."

She opened a new message to the woman and typed out a brief introduction before taking a picture of the watch and sending it. When she was done, her message read, *Hi, my name is Tulia Blake. I am staying at the same bed and breakfast as your nephew, Matthew Jameson, was. I found this watch on a path by the loch, and I think it belongs to him, but I would like to confirm it with you before I turn it over to the police to be sent home with the rest of his belongings. Do you recognize it?*

"There, now we can do is –" She broke off as a response made her computer ding almost instantly.

I do recognize it, the message said. *That belonged to Matthew's grandfather. He inherited it, along with a lot of his grandfather's things, a few months ago. I'm not sure when he will be home. Did he leave the bed and breakfast already? Can you mail it directly to me? He is supposed to come and visit me before going home, so I can probably return it to him more quickly than the local police can. I'm happy to pay you for the trouble. Thank you so much for reaching out instead of keeping it.*

Tulia stared at the message for a long moment, her stomach sinking. "It looks like she doesn't know he's dead," she said slowly. "Look at this, she's talking like he's still coming home at some point."

Samuel frowned. "That's unfortunate. I'm not sure if we should tell her or just leave it be. I can't imagine why the rest of the family hasn't reached out to her. They seem close online."

"I'd feel terrible letting her believe something like this. She's going to go on thinking he's still alive until she gets a call from the rest of her family. I feel like we should say something."

"I don't think there is a right answer here. Maybe you're right, it seems cruel to act like he's fine when we know he isn't. Just... be gentle."

She nodded and focused on her keyboard as she typed out the words.

I am so sorry, Catherine. Matthew passed away a couple of days ago. The local police should have notified his family already. I hate having to give you this news. I'm going to give the watch to the local police, since they might be able to use it in the investigation into his death. You have my deepest condolences for your loss.

She sent the message off, her stomach twisting. It took almost a minute for the woman to respond this time, though she could see the dots coming up in the message app screen letting her know that Catherine was typing.

You're very kind, but I'm glad to say you are mistaken about his death. There was an error with the police station up in Scotland, and they falsely reported it. I'm glad to say my nephew is alive and well. I talked to him just earlier today. I'm a little surprised that he isn't still there for you to hand the watch back in person. Please do mail it to me. He is planning on coming here to visit before returning to New York. It's been a few years since I've seen him, and I'm thrilled to finally see him.

Tulia exchanged a look with Samuel. Something was deeply wrong here. There was no way she had spoken to Matthew. Tulia had seen his body herself.

I don't know how to say this, she typed, *but I witnessed his death. Something confusing is going on. Are you sure it was him you talked to? Did you see him on a video call, or just hear his voice?*

The response came back quickly, and Tulia got a

feeling the person typing on the other end was beginning to get angry.

No, I didn't see him on a video call. I just talked to him. I think I know my own nephew's voice, though, and I certainly know his cell phone number. Please stop sending me these horrible messages. I'm taking screenshots of this conversation, and I will notify the police if you end up keeping his watch.

Tulia grimaced. *Please, if you don't believe me, try to get him on a video call. I am telling you, something is wrong here. I can guarantee you that Matthew is no longer at the bed and breakfast. He passed away on the boat, to the best of my knowledge. I really do hope there was some sort of mix-up and the hospital was able to revive him, but I highly doubt it. Just be careful, and be aware that whoever you're talking to could be a scammer.*

There was no reply after that. Tulia waited for nearly twenty minutes before finally shutting her laptop with a sigh. "That... could have been better. I feel horrible."

"You were right to warn her," Samuel said. "We both know Matthew Jameson is dead. But if someone really did call his aunt from his phone, then something more is going on here."

Tulia was beginning to feel like they might have

gotten in over their heads. She stared at the golden watch where it sat innocently on the table. She was no longer certain what to do with it. Giving it to the police seemed like the best option, but how long would it take them to get it back to his family? She decided to hold onto it for now, just until she knew more about what was going on.

CHAPTER TEN

They stayed in their room until dinner. Samuel decided to ask Marc to run a quick background check on Matthew, since there was something strange going on with the reports of his death. Marc told them he would get the information back to them by tomorrow. After that, Tulia got on a quick video call with her parents, giving them a more upbeat update as to how the trip was going. She missed them – moving to Massachusetts had meant moving away from where they lived in Michigan, and she had only managed to visit them once since her move a few months ago. She carefully kept her left hand with the engagement ring on it out of sight of the camera. She was planning on visiting them in person again soon, and wanted to save that particular surprise for then.

She felt bad that Matthew's death had overshadowed excitement about being engaged to Samuel, but she could always celebrate later. Matthew, on the other hand, would never get a second chance at life. She still didn't know if his death had been a homicide or an accident, but there was something odd about his missing belongings and the story his aunt had told them.

When Gwen called them down to supper, she was a little surprised to see that both Chloe and Ryan were there in the dining room. They were sitting on opposite ends of the table, and seemed to be ignoring each other. Christopher was there as well, already halfway through his plate of fish and chips. Tulia paused by the doorway, realizing this might be their best chance to talk to Gwen.

"Is everything all right, dear?" the older woman asked.

"Actually, do you think we could talk to you briefly first?" Tulia asked. The watch felt heavy in her pocket. She just wanted to get this over with.

Gwen nodded and led them into the kitchen. The sink was stacked with the dishes that had been used to cook dinner, and a freshly made coffeecake was cooling on the counter. Tulia wondered if that was going to be for breakfast, but quickly refocused on what she was going to say as Samuel leaned against the counter next to her.

"I'm sure you remember what Chloe accused Ewan of this morning," she said. "The issue with the watch she said belongs to Matthew. While we were at the picnic, Samuel and I both thought we saw a gold watch on Ewan's wrist. We went back out there later and found this tossed off alongside the path." She took the watch out of her pocket. "We did a little bit of research, and the initials on it prove that it belonged to Matthew's grandfather. I'd like to contact the police about this, but I wanted to let you know first. Have you ever had any other issues like this with Ewan?"

Gwen stared at the watch, her eyes wide.

"No," she said slowly. "No, he's always been a great employee. Not always the hardest worker, but he's gotten better over the years. I just can't believe this. Not that I'm saying I think you're lying, but I've known the lad for years." She took a deep breath. "I suppose this means he stole the other items out of Matthew's room as well. You said you're going to the police?"

Samuel nodded. "It's the right thing to do. We were just letting you know first as a courtesy."

"Well, Ewan has already gone home for the

evening. Can you wait to call them until the morning, when he's here? I want a chance to ask him about this first. I just feel the need to talk to him, to ask him why he did this. I feel so betrayed. I knew his family, you see. I knew him as a small, wee child. This isn't like him at all. Of course, if you need to call the police right away, I understand, but it would mean a lot to me if you could wait until the morning."

Tulia hesitated, exchanging a glance with Samuel. He frowned. "I'm afraid that if this gets out somehow, he will use the extra time to hide any more stolen items he might have."

Gwen mimed zipping her lips. "I won't say a peep, I promise. I'll even wait until after you contact the police to start asking him questions. I just... well, imagine if it was someone you had known for many years. Wouldn't you want to a chance to ask them *why*?"

Samuel sighed. He looked over at Tulia again, who shrugged. She knew it would probably be best to call the police right away, but she could also understand why Gwen wanted them to wait.

"We'll wait," Samuel decided. "We're going to call first thing in the morning."

"I appreciate it," Gwen said. "Now, let's put our brave faces on and go eat some supper."

Tulia tucked the watch back into her pocket and the three of them filed into the dining room. Christopher was engaged in a conversation with Ryan about Santa Barbara, where Ryan and Chloe were from.

"Yeah, it's pretty much a paradise," Ryan was saying. "If you can afford to live there, of course. It can get expensive, but I can't imagine living anywhere else. It's a world of difference from this place. It's so dreary here."

"It sounds great," Christopher said, smiling. "I'd love to live somewhere it doesn't rain almost every day."

"The city itself might be nice, but the people there suck," Chloe snapped from across the table. "That's where I met Ryan, after all."

Ryan shot her a sharp glare, which she returned. Gwen sat down quickly and said, "No arguing at the dinner table, please."

Tulia served herself a plate of fish and fries – well, chips, as they were called here. There was some malted vinegar that she was supposed to sprinkle on top. It was a good meal, a bit heavy on the fried food for her tastes, but definitely delicious. There wasn't much conversation as they ate. After a few minutes, Christopher pushed back his empty plate and said,

"Thanks again for letting me stay here, Gwen. I'll be out of your hair in the morning."

"Don't you go running off without finishing the rest of that work you owe me," Gwen warned. "I've been giving you three free meals a day. I expect fair labor in return."

"I'll leave some money in the carriage house for you," Christopher said. "That should be all right, shouldn't it?"

Gwen looked a little puzzled. "I suppose it's none of my business, if you can afford it. You *have* been a good guest, just leave the place in a good condition. Please strip the sheets off of the bed you used. And if you could take your plate into the kitchen, I would appreciate it."

Christopher nodded and rose, taking his plate with him as he left the dining room. Chloe stood up suddenly too, grabbing her own plate.

"I'm leaving tomorrow as well," she said. "I'm going to take a bus to London and spend the rest of my trip there. I already talked to Ryan and he promised to pay the rest of what we owe you. Thank you for hosting such a nice bed and breakfast. I'm sorry I won't be staying longer too, but there's no way I'm going to spend the rest of my vacation trapped in the same building as my ex."

With that, she left the room, pausing to shoo the two golden retrievers away before they could get in and start begging for food. Ryan winced a little as Gwen gave him a sympathetic look.

"This has been a hard week for everyone," she said, then looked at Tulia and Samuel. "What about the two of you? Are you going to be staying out the week?"

"I think so," Tulia said. "Despite everything, we have been having a nice time here. This really is a beautiful place you have."

Gwen gave her a warm smile. "It has its ups and downs, but I hope one day you'll come back and see how peaceful and relaxing it usually is here. I wouldn't trade this life for the world."

CHAPTER ELEVEN

After dinner, they returned to their room and decided to watch a movie online before bed. They settled into the loveseat, broke open some of the snacks they bought the first time they went into the village, threw a crocheted blanket over their laps, and found something to stream on her laptop.

Just a few minutes after the movie started, Tulia paused it, looking at Samuel with raised eyebrows. "I just realized, the internet here isn't bad at all. I had those video chats with Violet and my parents, and now we're streaming a movie with no issues. What on earth was Christopher talking about having bad internet here? He shouldn't have had to go into town to do something on his computer."

Samuel's eyebrows pulled together. "Now that

you bring it up, that's a good point. I'm not sure. Maybe the signal isn't as strong in the carriage house, and it just didn't occur to him to try using the Wi-Fi in the main building."

"That might explain it," she said as she hit play again. It still seemed a little strange to her, but she figured it was also possible that Christopher just wanted a chance to get away from everyone. This probably hadn't been the relaxing stay he had hoped for. It hadn't been what any of them had hoped for.

She woke up bright and early, knowing that today was the day they would call the police about the watch Ewan had stolen. After getting dressed, she and Samuel went downstairs. The watch was in her pocket again, and she felt a little bad that she wasn't mailing it to Catherine like the woman had asked. This was the right way to go about it, though. She was sure the police would get it back to his family eventually.

Gwen had slices of coffeecake sitting on the front desk and offered them each a piece along with mugs of hot coffee. The two dogs were looking at the cake longingly, but seemed well trained enough not to try to snatch it off the desk. Tulia caught her eye and Gwen grimaced at the serious expression on her face.

"He's here. He is just finishing up the dishes in the kitchen. I'll talk to him after. You can go ahead and make the call as soon as you're done with your coffeecake."

They picked up their plates and sat in the small reading nook together, their knees bumping. As they were sitting down, the door to the bed and breakfast opened and Chloe came in. "I've just got one more suitcase to grab," she told Gwen. "The bus won't be late, will it? I don't want to wait around for too long."

"It will arrive at nine or a few minutes after," Gwen assured her. "Have you seen Christopher? I was hoping to offer him some coffeecake as well, but he hasn't been in yet this morning."

"I heard him on a phone call inside the carriage house," Chloe said. "It sounded like he was trying to use an American accent, for some reason. Made me laugh. Anyway, he'll probably stop in to say goodbye before he leaves."

She walked back through the bed and breakfast toward her room. Tulia took her first bite of the moist coffeecake, sparing a moment to admire Gwen's skills in the kitchen. The woman could cook, there was no doubt about that.

She was only halfway through with her slice when Ewan came out of the kitchen and approached Gwen at the front desk.

"What do you want me to do next?" he asked.

"Has Chloe gotten all of her things out of her room yet?"

"No, not yet," Gwen said. "It'll probably be a few more minutes. Hold on, though. There's something I wanted to ask you."

She looked past him to nod at Tulia, who froze. For some reason, she hadn't expected Gwen to bring her into this. She thought she and Samuel would just call the police, tell them what they had found, then hand the watch over and be done with it all. Instead, Gwen gestured for her to come closer.

"Remember the watch Chloe thought she saw you wearing the other day? Well, Tulia here found something interesting when she and Samuel went back to that little lake. Tulia? Please show him what you found."

Reluctantly, Tulia stood up and took the watch out of her pocket. Ewan stared at it, his face going pale. "I've never seen that before in my life," he said quickly.

"Tulia, Chloe, and I all spotted this exact watch on your wrist during the picnic," Samuel said, coming over to stand next to Tulia. "It's not worth lying about. Where did you get it?"

Ewan looked between them, his expression frantic. After a second, he seemed to deflate. "I found it in Matthew's room."

Gwen looked deeply saddened. "So it was you who stole his things, wasn't it?"

"I didn't think it would hurt anyone," Ewan said, defensive. "It's a victimless crime. He was already dead, it's not as if he was going to use any of it. The police were just going to take it and it would all end up in evidence for the next decade. I thought I could sell some of it and keep the rest. I wasn't hurting anyone by doing it. And they already took all the important stuff out, anyway."

"They weren't going to take anything until the next morning," Tulia said. "I don't think they even went upstairs that day."

He frowned. "What are you talking about? All of his personal belongings – his laptop, cell phone, even his passport and IDs, were all gone. I know he didn't have all of that on the boat with him. His phone, maybe, but not the rest. I wasn't going to take any of that, I knew the police would need it for their investigation. I just took a few things, like the watch, some of his nicer suits, and a bunch of little souvenirs he'd bought."

"It's still wrong," Gwen said, putting her hands on her hips. "I'm unbelievably disappointed in you,

Ewan. I've gone out of my way to make this a good place for you to work, and this is how you repay me after all of these years…"

She continued haranguing him, but Tulia and Samuel slipped back into the reading nook and sat down so they could talk quietly, their heads close together as they whispered.

"Do you think he's telling the truth?" Tulia asked. "About not taking any of Matthew's important technology or belongings?"

"I don't know. I don't see why he would lie, it seems like a strange thing for him to bring up if he did take it."

She frowned again, but then her phone dinged with an incoming message. She checked the screen, surprised to find a message from Catherine, Matthew's aunt who she had contacted the day before.

I wanted to let you know, I just got off a video call with my nephew. It's definitely him. He's perfectly fine. Please stop spreading these horrible lies. His family has already been through enough. Please return the watch to us ASAP, and then cease all contact with me.

She showed the message to Samuel, who read it with increasing confusion on his face.

"This doesn't make any sense," Samuel said. "We

both *saw* that he was dead. The ambulance took him away in a body bag, for goodness sakes. There is no way the person she talked to was her nephew."

"Well, either this lady is completely insane, or something really strange is going on," Tulia said. She wracked her mind, wondering how someone had tricked Catherine into thinking she was talking to her nephew.

Then Chloe's words came back to her. Christopher had just been on a call in the carriage house, trying to use an American accent.

Christopher, who suddenly seemed to have more money than he should have, whose mood had improved greatly since Matthew's death, and who was Matthew's doppelgänger.

She inhaled sharply. "Samuel, I think I know what's going on. We need to make sure Christopher doesn't leave. I think he murdered Matthew, and is trying to steal his identity."

CHAPTER TWELVE

"I'm ringing the police, Ewan," Gwen said as Samuel and Tulia stepped out of the reading nook again. "I'm sorry, but I have to do it. What you did is a crime, and I need to alert the authorities. You are going to go sit down and wait for them. I don't want to hear a peep of complaint out of you."

"No, please," Ewan said. "I'll return everything I took. It was a stupid decision. I know I shouldn't have done it."

"Ewan," Tulia said, getting his attention. "Are you telling the truth about his passport and laptop and other personal items? You really didn't take them?"

He nodded frantically. "Yes! I swear, I am. That's why I thought the police had already been there and taken everything important. I didn't touch any of that."

"Gwen, please do call the police. I think something more is going on here. We've been in contact with Matthew's aunt, and she swears she just got off a video call with her nephew. Of course, we know that's impossible. We think Christopher has something to do with this. He's the only one who looks enough like Matthew to pull it off, and he would have been able to slip upstairs and steal Matthews identification and laptop before Ewan took his other things. He could even have taken his cell phone, back on the boat."

Gwen paled even further she hurried around to the back of the desk to grab the phone. Samuel opened the bed and breakfast's door. "We're going to make sure he doesn't leave before they get here," he said.

They stepped outside to see that Christopher was already loading his backpack and a few other things into the back of his rental car. He looked up when he saw them and waved, though the smile on his face fell at the sight of their grim expressions. Behind them, the bed and breakfast door opened again. Tulia turned, expecting to see Gwen or Ewan coming out, but it was just Chloe. She was dragging a suitcase behind her and put it in a row with her other luggage.

She turned and looked at them, raising an eyebrow. "What?"

"You might want to go back inside," Tulia said before hurrying to catch up with Samuel, who was already approaching Christopher.

"You're going to need to wait around for a second," Samuel said.

"What on earth for?" Christopher said. "I have a flight to catch."

"A flight?" Samuel raised his eyebrows. "I thought you couldn't even afford to stay in a bed and breakfast. Where did you get all of this money so quickly?"

Christopher shook his head and gave a stilted laugh. "Did I say flight? I meant, I've got a long drive ahead of me. I am heading back to London early. Why do you want me to wait around? There's nothing for me here."

Samuel hesitated, and Tulia wasn't sure what to say either. If they let him know the police were on their way, he might use that as an excuse to take off early. But it looked like he was done packing. She glanced through the open door into the carriage house and saw that the bedding had been stripped off the bed and everything was already tidy. He was just about ready to go.

"We discovered who stole Matthew's belongings," Samuel said slowly. "You're going to need to give a statement to the police about it. It was the man who works here, Ewan."

Christopher's expression seemed to relax a little.

"Oh," he said. "Is that all? Yeah, I don't think I need to wait around for that. I didn't see anything, and I need to get going."

"What's the hurry?" Tulia said. "They should be here in just a few minutes. The village isn't far away, and I can't imagine they're very busy."

"Why do you care so much if I stay?" he snapped.

Chloe wandered over, looking intrigued. "What's going on?"

"I'm going to be late for my flight, that's what," Christopher retorted, crossing his arms.

"I thought you said you didn't have a flight to catch," Tulia said.

He winced. "Fine, I came into some money, okay? I have to go catch a flight, and I can't miss it. I don't have to time to wait around for the police."

"Why are the police coming?" Chloe asked.

"We found out Ewan is the one who stole most of Matthew's things," Tulia told her.

"It has nothing to do with me, so I don't see why I need to stay," Christopher said.

"He really does have a flight to catch," Chloe said. "I also don't want to hang around and wait for them. None of us saw him do anything, so it's not like we'll be of any help to the investigation. I'm certainly not going to miss my bus if it gets here before the police arrive."

"Thank you," Christopher said to her. "They're being completely unreasonable."

"How do you know about his flight?" Samuel asked Chloe.

She shrugged. "I was just making sure there were no loose ends left with Ryan. He's going to swing by our place back home to pick up his things after the trip. He mentioned to me that he managed to get Christopher to agree to fly out to Santa Barbara for a visit. Of course, he added in a few barbs about me cheating on him, since he looks almost like Matthew and apparently I have a 'type.'" She made air quotes. "But my point is, he's not lying about that, so you'd better let him go."

It was slowly coming together for Tulia. Catherine lived in California. Christopher probably thought it was a good idea to visit her to solidify his identity as Matthew. He looked just similar enough to Matthew that she might not realize the difference, since it had been so long since she had seen her nephew. If he was practicing an American accent, he just might be able to pull it off. Having a family member who could confirm that "Matthew" was alive, it would probably keep the rest of Matthew's family off his back for a while. If he had access to all of Matthew's money, he could easily pick up and disappear before they realized something was wrong.

"It's convenient, you coming into money like that," Samuel said.

"It happens," Christopher said. He shrugged, an amused smile coming to his face. "My grandfather died, as a matter of fact. I've inherited everything. He was American, so I might spend some time over there."

It seemed like he was already working some pieces of Matthew's identity into his story. Tulia grimaced, but she wasn't sure what to do. She didn't want to let him know they were onto him, but she also didn't want to let him leave. If he used Matthew's ID to buy the plane ticket and board the plane, the police might not be able to track down the right person in time.

To her surprise, Chloe moved forward, frowning.

"No, you didn't," she said. "The first night we were here, you told us that you didn't have any family left. Your dad ran off when you were younger, your mom had some mental health issues and is in a care facility, and all four of your grandparents passed away when you were a child."

He hesitated. "Well, what I meant was the last one had just died. You must have misheard me. Now, I've got to give this to Gwen." He raised an envelope between two fingers. "It's the money I owe her. I'm leaving after that."

He slammed the trunk shut and strode past them, toward the bed and breakfast. Samuel turned to watch him go, his arms crossed. Tulia bit her lip as he entered the building. There was no way to stop him. Maybe she could take a picture of the rental car's license plate and the police could use that to track him down. She turned on her cell phone and turned back to the rental car, only to see Chloe opening the driver's side door. She hit a button and the trunk popped open. Tulia blinked. Chloe looked at her over the roof of the car and shrugged. She went around to the trunk and pulled open Christopher's backpack. Tulia approached cautiously.

"What are you doing?

"Something weird's going on, and I want to get to the bottom of this," Chloe said. "I'm not an idiot, you know. Christopher's been acting strange ever since Matthew died, and before you two got here, he kept commenting on how similar they looked. And I swear, I saw him standing near Matthew a minute or two before he fell into the lake. I've been wondering if he had anything to do with it for a while, but I couldn't think of a reason he would want to kill him, and I really did think it was probably an accident. But all this money stuff is super shady." She made a noise of triumph and pulled a passport out of the ragged backpack. She flipped it open and they came face-to-face with Matthew's picture and name. She held it up, her eyes glinting. "This is Matthew's."

Slowly, Tulia took the passport. There was no doubt about who it belonged to. Examining his photo, she could find a few small differences between his and Christopher's faces, but at a glance, they looked identical. She turned back to Samuel and gave him the passport, which he examined closely.

"What are you doing?" Christopher asked as he came back out of the bed and breakfast. Gwen was beside him, a look of concern on her face. Honey and Heather, the two Golden retrievers, were both sitting calmly beside her. She had the envelope of cash clutched in one hand.

"We found everything out," Tulia said, crossing her arms. "We know you're trying to steal Matthew's identity."

Christopher froze, his face going pale. "Is that a passport? I don't know how that got there. You have no proof I took it."

"Actually, I think we do," Tulia said. "You don't know this, but we've been talking to Matthew's aunt, Catherine. She told us that she just got off a video chat with someone who looked like her nephew, and Chloe overheard you on a call in your carriage house trying to talk with an American accent. I'm sure Catherine would be more than happy to testify to the police about the call, and I'm sure if they trace the origins of the call, they'll find out it came from here. One way or another, they're going to put things together. It's over, Christopher."

Christopher slowly backed away, a look of despair coming over his face.

"You can't do this to me," he said. "I was so close. You don't know what it's like to have nothing. I just wanted to make things better for myself."

"There's one last thing we're curious about," Samuel said. "Did you kill him, or was it really an accident?"

"Oh, it wasn't an accident," Gwen said, giving Christopher a dirty look as she backed away from him. "The police took a fire extinguisher off the boat. It had been taken off the exterior wall of the cabin and it was all dented up. There were specks of blood still on it. The constable told me all about it. Matthew was murdered. They just asked me to keep it quiet while they built a case."

Christopher paled, looking between them and then glancing at his car. Both Tulia and Samuel stood between him and it, and Chloe walked up beside Tulia, the car's keys dangling from her fingers.

"You left these in the ignition," she said, twirling them around. "Kind of reckless for someone who might need to make a quick getaway, don't you think?"

He was trapped. Even if he tried to run now, the police would catch him before he got far on foot.

He had tried to steal a man's identity, but all he had done in the end was destroy his own future for good.

EPILOGUE

"I think next spring is fine," Violet said. The two of them were at their favorite sushi restaurant while Samuel and Marc filed paperwork for their latest case. Tulia had already been home for a week, and it had been great to see Cicero again and ease back into her life in Loon Bay. With all the chaos and intrigue of Matthew's murder behind them, she could finally focus on the matter at hand – her engagement to Samuel.

She had gotten a few emails from Gwen with updates on the case. Christopher had admitted to tricking Matthew into letting him hold his cell phone, and had then swung the fire extinguisher at the back of his head, killing him instantly and sending his body into the loch. He had scrambled to get all of the man's identification and his laptop stashed away in his backpack, and had spent his day out in town hacking into all of his accounts and contacting Matthew's family to pretend his victim was still alive. With access to the man's money, he had rented a car and later, booked a flight to the US, where he was planning on starting his stolen life.

She hated thinking about how close he had been to succeeding, and did her best to push the thoughts of the case out of her mind now.

"You don't think it's too soon?" Tulia asked. "We just got engaged, that will only be about, what, six or seven months from now?"

"I think it will be fine. Do it late spring. Maybe sometime in May? Are you guys having a destination wedding?"

Tulia nodded. "We've been talking about it. Neither of us really want a long engagement – we would like to buy a house together and basically start building our future together, and we both want to be married before we do that. We think a destination wedding would be perfect, since we met while we were traveling and it's been a big part of our lives. But I'm going to offer to pay everyone's airfare and hotel stay, or rent a big building where everyone can stay together. I can afford it, and I don't want anyone to struggle to pay if they want to go, or feel as if they can't go because they can't afford it."

"I think that's really kind of you," Violet said. "Do you know yet where you're having it?"

"We're thinking about Nantucket Island," she said. "It's not too far from here, but neither of us has ever been. And they have some lovely wedding venues. It's going to be a little bit of a rush to get a venue reserved in time and make all the other arrangements, but I think it'll be worth it. I know my parents have always wanted to go there, and I've always been interested in visiting as well."

"That will be great," Violet said. "I've always loved Nantucket. You'll want to check the weather to make sure it's warm enough – maybe early summer would be better – but I just know you're going to have the perfect wedding. Oh, I'm so excited for you, Tulia. I know you are a little worried about how quickly you and Samuel are moving, but you two are perfect together. I'm so happy that he finally found someone – and that you did too, of course."

Tulia grinned. "Thanks. I'm pretty happy myself. I wanted to ask you, though, would you be one of my bridesmaids? I think I'm also going to ask Angela – one of the first friends I made on my big road trip –

and maybe a few other people, but I'm not going to have a huge wedding party."

"I would love to be a bridesmaid," Violet said. "And if you need someone to wrangle your bird for you during the wedding, I'd be happy to do that too. I'm guessing you want to have Cicero there?"

She grinned. "Of course. It wouldn't feel right without him. I might even try to find someone who will make a little tuxedo for him, though I'm not sure whether I'll be able to convince him to wear it."

She took a bite of her sushi with a pair of chopsticks and felt contentment settle over her like a warm blanket. Everything had changed for her in these past two years, but she couldn't imagine being happier. Marrying Samuel was just one more step in the adventure of her life.